Written by David Bedford
Illustrated by Brenna Vaughan and Henry St. Leger

First published 2013 by Parragon Books, Ltd.
Copyright © 2018 Cottage Door Press, LLC
5005 Newport Drive, Rolling Meadows, Illinois 60008
All Rights Reserved

10 9 8 7 6 5 4 3 2 1

ISBN 978-1-68052-540-3

Parragon Books is an imprint of Cottage Door Press, LLC.
Parragon Books® and the Parragon® logo are
registered trademarks of Cottage Door Press, LLC.

I love my Grandma

PaRragon.

Little Hedgehog and Grandma Hedgehog
loved to play hide-and-seek together.
One day, when Grandma went to find
Little Hedgehog ...

Little Hedgehog hid! He put his paws over his mouth so that Grandma couldn't hear him giggling.

"Where, oh where can Little Hedgehog be?"
said Grandma. "I want to make a yummy
picnic, and I need help."
Little Hedgehog giggled again.

"Oh, well," said Grandma. "I will have
to make the picnic myself."
Little Hedgehog followed closely
behind Grandma.

"I wish Little Hedgehog were here to help me pick juicy blackberries," said Grandma.

When she wasn't looking, Little Hedgehog picked the **biggest blackberries** he could reach … and put them into Grandma's basket!

"What a lot of berries!" said Grandma, surprised. "I already have enough for baking."

Little Hedgehog scampered into Grandma's kitchen to find the best place to hide.

Little Hedgehog crouched down low
so that Grandma couldn't see him.

"If only Little Hedgehog were here to help me!" said Grandma.

Little Hedgehog giggled again. Then he licked his lips as Grandma
Hedgehog poured sweet, scrumptious honey into her mixing bowl.

"Honey is my treat for Little Hedgehog," said Grandma.
Little Hedgehog crept out from his hiding place …

He tried not to make a sound as he tasted the honey for himself, but it was too good!

"Yum!"
whispered Little Hedgehog.

Then he hurried back to his hiding place. Suddenly ...

"Aha!" said Grandma. "Someone has been tasting my honey! And they have left sticky footprints!"

"Oh, no!" Little Hedgehog didn't want to be found. Not yet!

Grandma followed the

teeny,

tiny,

sticky

footprints

across the kitchen.

"Someone has been playing hide-and-seek
with me!" she said, smiling. Then …

"I've found you, Little Hedgehog!" said Grandma.

But Little Hedgehog
wasn't behind the
rocking chair.

There were only more sticky footprints ...

Grandma followed the sticky footprints out of
the kitchen and into the yard.

The sticky footprints went around and around and stopped by the flowerpots.

"I've found you this time, Little Hedgehog!" said Grandma.

But Little Hedgehog wasn't
behind the flowerpots!
He was ... inside one!

"Surprise!"
said Little Hedgehog, giggling as
he gave Grandma a big hug.

"Wow, Little Hedgehog," said his grandma.
"You are the best at hide-and-seek. And I hope you are
hungry, because our picnic is ready!"

"I am hungry!" said Little Hedgehog. But when he looked around the yard, he couldn't see a picnic anywhere. "Where is it?" he asked. Grandma giggled.

"You have to find it!" she said.

Little Hedgehog searched
around the yard and
soon found …

honey cookies …

and fruit salad.

Then Grandma brought out a
giant blackberry and honey cake.

"Yum!"
said Little Hedgehog.
It was the best he had ever tasted.

"I love Grandma's picnics!"
Little Hedgehog shouted happily. "And …

"I love my grandma!"